THE HALLOWEEN CAPER

CONTENTS

Literacy Footprints, Inc.

CHAPTER 1
COSTUMES

"What are you guys going to be for Halloween?" Galaxy Girl asked Spaceboy and Space Monster.

"I'm going to be a cowboy," said Spaceboy. "Grandpa has a cool cowboy hat I can wear."

"What about you, Space Monster?" asked Galaxy Girl. "Do you know what you're going to be?"

Space Monster shrugged.

"We can help you think
of something," said Galaxy Girl.
"I'm going to be a dog. I'm making a
hat with doggy ears and a suit with a
long tail."

"You could be a cowboy like me,"
said Spaceboy to Space Monster.
"Or, how about a pumpkin?
I could paint you orange!"

"That would be a little messy,"
said Galaxy Girl.
"I have a ghost costume I wore
last year. You'd make a good ghost,
Space Monster."

Space Monster nodded happily.
He jumped in a puddle and then made
small monster footprints on the sidewalk.

On Halloween night everyone
put on their costumes.
They all went from house to house
trick-or-treating. Soon their bags
were filled with candy.

"Spaceboy, I hope you're not
going to eat all your candy tonight,"
said Galaxy Girl. "Remember
how sick you were last year."

Spaceboy groaned. "Yes, I remember!"

All of a sudden, Pluto Boy and two
of his friends jumped out
from behind some bushes.
They were all dressed up like pirates.

"Hey, Space Monster.
Really scary costume,"
said Pluto Boy in a jeering voice.

"Yeah, real scary,"
said the other pirates.

CHAPTER 2
THE SNATCH

Pluto Boy looked
at Space Monster's bag. "Looks like
you got a lot of booty there.
Too bad you ran into pirates!"
Pluto Boy grabbed the bag
with his hook and then turned
and began running down the sidewalk
with the other pirate boys.

"Hey!" said Spaceboy.

"Stop, you bully," yelled Galaxy Girl.

"Don't worry Space Monster,"
said Galaxy Girl. "We'll share our candy
with you. We have plenty."

Space Monster sniffed from under
his costume. Galaxy Girl and
Spaceboy knew he was trying not to cry.

"I wish there was a way to get back
at that bully," said Galaxy Girl.
"He just makes me so mad!"

Spaceboy took off his cowboy hat
and scratched his head.
"I think I have an idea," he said.
"Come on."

They left Space Monster at his house
and then walked to Spaceboy's house.
"How was trick-or-treating?"
asked Spaceboy's mother.

"Fine," said Spaceboy.
"I need some cardboard. Do we have
any large pieces of cardboard?"

When they got to Spaceboy's room Galaxy Girl said, "What are we doing with the cardboard? What's your idea?"

"You'll see,"
said Spaceboy mysteriously.

CHAPTER 3
A BIG MONSTER

Galaxy Girl watched while Spaceboy
drew and then cut out
two large feet, one right
and one left. The feet looked
just like Space Monster's feet,
only five times bigger.

"Hey," said Galaxy Girl. "They look like
huge, monster feet."

"Exactly," said Spaceboy. "And next,
I need some mud."

They made mud by mixing
some dirt from the garden
with water. They put the mud
in a bucket.

"Let's go," said Spaceboy.

Galaxy Girl followed Spaceboy
to Pluto Boy's house.

Spaceboy took the left monster foot and dipped it in the mud. Then he carefully placed it down on the walk. He did the same thing with the right foot. Soon there were huge monster footprints going up the walk to Pluto Boy's house.

In the morning Spaceboy and Galaxy Girl watched Pluto Boy come out of his house. He stopped and stared at the huge footprints on the walk. They looked like Space Monster's feet, only bigger. Spaceboy and Galaxy Girl walked up. "Do you see these footprints?" asked Pluto Boy.

"Hmm," said Spaceboy.
"They look like Space Monster's
 big brother's footprints."

"His big brother?" said Pluto Boy.

"Yes," said Galaxy Girl.
"His big brother lives down
 in the swamp. He only comes out
 when he is really upset."

"Uh, oh," said Spaceboy.
"I'd watch out. He's pretty scary
 when he's upset!"

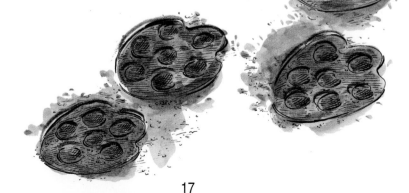

At school Spaceboy and Galaxy Girl
told Space Monster what they had done.
Space Monster frowned.
"But I don't want the boys and girls
to be afraid of me—or my family."

Spaceboy and Galaxy Girl looked
at each other.

"Lots of kids are scared of me
because I look different. Remember
when you were scared of me?"
Space Monster asked them.

Then Pluto Boy ran in.
He dropped a bag
onto Space Monster's desk.
"Here's your candy back,"
Pluto Boy told Space Monster.

"Tell your brother it was just
a little Halloween prank.
I never planned to keep it."

Space Monster looked at the bag.
He reached in and pulled out
some candy bars and handed them
to Pluto Boy. "Here," he said.

Pluto Boy backed up.
"Why are you giving me those?"
asked Pluto Boy. "I took your candy!"

"Do you like chocolate?"
asked Space Monster.

"Umm, yes. Thanks," said Pluto Boy.
He scratched his head and then
shrugged and ate the chocolate.
He started to walk away
and then came back.
He reached in his lunch bag.
"And here is something for you—
a strawberry lollipop. It's really good."

Space Monster took the lollipop.
"Thanks!" he said. He smiled
at Pluto Boy. "Strawberry is my favorite!"

Cheerios®

Action Park Adventure

by Justine Fontes
illustrated by Mada Design

ISBN 0-439-70343-3

Published by Scholastic Inc.
SCHOLASTIC and associated logos are trademarks
and/or registered trademarks of Scholastic Inc.

12 11 10 9 8 7 6 5 4 3 2 1   5 6 7 8 9 10

Printed in the U.S.A.
First printing, February 2005

SCHOLASTIC INC.

New York   Toronto   London   Auckland   Sydney
Mexico City   New Delhi   Hong Kong   Buenos Aires

"Have a good time!" says Michael's dad.

"Thank you," Lisa tells Michael. "You're so nice to spend your birthday 💵 taking us to the Action Park."

"I spent all my birthday 💵 on a 🦴 for my new 🐕," says Ben.

"Come on!" says Michael. "I want to ride the 🎢!"

"Oh, no!" says Michael. "I forgot my birthday 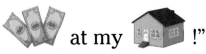 at my ! !"

"Don't worry," says Lisa. "We'll put our  together."

"Good idea," says Michael. "Now we have enough to buy for the rides. Some rides cost only 1 . The bigger rides cost more."

Ben's , Noodle, barks. "I hope they let ride free," says Ben.

Everyone laughs.

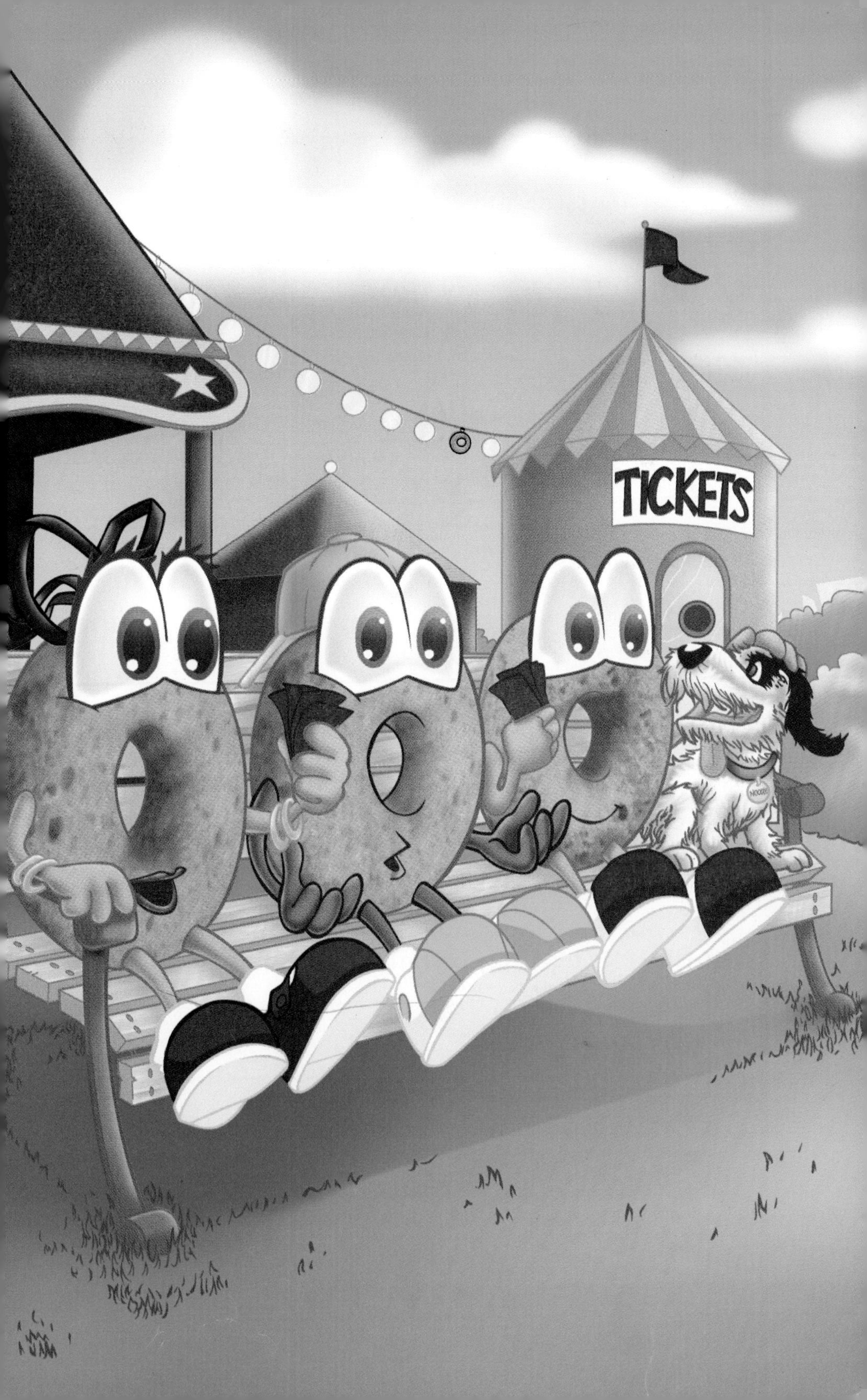
TICKETS

"I want to ride the 🎡," says Lisa. She counts her 🎟️: "I have 1 + 1 + 1 + 1 + 1. That's 5 🎟️."

"How many more 🎟️ do you need?" asks Ben.

"The 🎡 costs 7 🎟️," says Michael. "Lisa has 5. I can give her 1 of my 🎟️. Now she has 6."

"I can give her 1 more 🎟️," says Ben. "Now she has 7. That is enough!"

"Smile!" says Lisa at the top of the 🎡. "My 📷 takes great 🖼️!"

5 + 1 + 1 = 7

"That was fun!" says Lisa when the ride ends.

Michael wants to ride the 🎢 , but he

doesn't want to use up all the 🎟️ . "Let's

ride the 🚂 that goes around the park,"

he says. "The 🚂 doesn't cost *any* 🎟️ ."

"Are there 🌭 on the 🚂 ?" Ben asks.

"You can't be hungry yet!" Lisa says. "We just

ate breakfast."

Ben laughs. "I'm always hungry."

Noodle barks. "Noodle is always hungry, too,"

says Ben.

Michael says, "Maybe you should have named

him Hungry."

On the 🚂 , Michael, Ben, and Lisa can

see the whole park.

"There's the 🎢 !" says Michael.

"There are places that sell 🌭 !" says Ben.

"Can we please get something to eat?

I'm hungry!"

"We can buy food here," says Lisa. " 🌭 cost

6 🎟️ ."

"There are 3 of us," says Ben. "3 🌭 times

6 🎟️ . That's 6 + 6 + 6 or 18 🎟️ ."

"We won't have many 🎟️ left for rides,"

Michael says.

"Wait a minute," says Ben. "Where's Noodle?"

6 + 6 + 6 = 18

"I dropped Noodle's 🐄," says Ben.

"He's lost!"

"How can we find him?" asks Michael.

"Let's go back on the 🚂," says Lisa.

"Maybe we'll see Noodle as we ride the 🚂."

"Look! Over there!" says Michael.

"It's Noodle! On the !" says Lisa.

"Noodle!"

"He doesn't hear us," says Ben. "Let's get off the at the next stop!"

"Look!" cries Lisa when they get off the

. "There's Noodle. Now he's on the log

flume ride!"

"I have to go on the log flume and get him!"

says Ben.

"The log flume costs 6 ," says Michael.

"I have only 4," Ben says. "I don't have

enough."

"I saved my last 7 to ride the ,"

says Michael. "But Noodle is more important.

Take 2 of mine. Now you have 6!"

"Thanks, Michael," says Ben. "You're a good

friend."

Ben spends his 6 and gets in line.

Then he hears a sound.

4 + 2 = 6

"Woof!"

"Noodle!" cries Ben. "You jumped off the log flume and found us!"

"I'm so glad he's back," says Michael. "I can ride the next year."

"At least we all had a good time," Ben says.

"I think Noodle had the most fun of all," says Lisa. She takes of him. Everyone laughs.

"Shall we ride the again?" Michael asks.

"Hi, everyone!" says Michael's dad. "Michael, I found your birthday at the . I thought you might need it."

Michael smiles. "Thanks, Dad. Now I can buy 60 ! Is that enough for *all* of us to ride the ?"

Ben says, "3 friends x 7 🎟️ = 21 🎟️."

"21 + 21 = 42 🎟️," says Lisa. "We can all ride the 🎢 *twice!*"

Ben says, "42 is 18 less than 60. We will have 18 🎟️ left. That's enough for Michael's dad to ride with us!"

Michael smiles again. "This adds up to the best birthday ever!"

21   +   21   =   42

Did you spot all the picture clues in this Cheerios reader?

Each picture clue is on a flash card.
Ask a grown-up to cut out the flash cards.
Then try reading the words on the back of the cards. The pictures will be your clue.

Reading and math are fun with Cheerios!

Just for fun!
Can you find a hidden Cheerio in each picture in the story?

bumper cars	camera
dog	Ferris wheel
house	hot dog

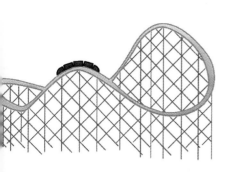

leash	money
pictures	roller coaster
tickets	train